To Lucienne
L. H.

ISBN 0-439-08188-2

Text copyright © 1995 by Martin Waddell.
Illustrations copyright © 1995 by Leo Hartas.
All rights reserved. Published by Scholastic Inc., 555 Broadway,
New York, NY 10012, by arrangement with Candlewick Press.
SCHOLASTIC and associated logos are trademarks and/or registered
trademarks of Scholastic Inc.

12 11 10 9 8 7 6 5 4 3 2 1   8 9/9 0 1 2 3/0

Printed in the U.S.A.   23

First Scholastic printing, April 1998

Mimi
and the
Picnic

Written by
MARTIN WADDELL
Illustrated by
LEO HARTAS

SCHOLASTIC INC.

New York Toronto London Auckland Sydney

Mexico City New Delhi Hong Kong

Mimi lived with her mouse sisters
and brothers beneath the big tree.
The mice came in all sizes, but the
smallest of all was called Hugo.

One day they all went for a picnic
on the bank of the river.

Mimi laid out a lovely lunch for her sisters and brothers.

Hugo sat on his Big Leaf and watched her, while the sisters and brothers ran off to play.

They played . . . and they played . . .

and they played . . .

and they played . . .

and they played . . .   and they played.

But when they came back for their lunch, Hugo's Big Leaf was empty. There was no sign of Hugo at all!

"Hugo's so small he'd be easily lost," Mimi said. "We'd better start looking for Hugo right away!"

The mouse sisters and brothers scurried about, under the leaves, and around Robin's Nest, and up Badger's Path by the two Rusty Tins, and down by Mole's Hole.

"Hugo's so small we can't find him at all,"
the mouse sisters and brothers told Mimi.
"Try looking some more!" Mimi said.

And they looked . . . and they looked . . .

and they looked . . .